The Golden Apple

THE GOLDEN APPLE

Text by Max Bolliger
translated by Roseanna Hoover

Pictures by Celestino Piatti

THE BODLEY HEAD
London · Sydney · Toronto

Once, in a clearing
in the middle of the forest, there stood
a great apple tree.
It was broader and taller
than any other tree.
It was
a giant apple tree.

It had many leaves,
all as big as platters.
But it had
just one apple.
That apple hung
on the highest branch,
near to the sun,
near to the moon,
near to the stars.

The apple was of gold.

One night a lion came through the forest
to the tree.
He saw the golden apple shining in the moonlight.
"Am I not the king of all the animals?"
said the lion.
"This apple belongs to me.
I will sit here under the tree
and wait
until the apple falls."

On the following night
an elephant came through the forest.
He saw the lion under the tree.
And he saw the golden apple shining in the moonlight.
"Am I not the largest of all the animals?"
said the elephant.
"This apple belongs to me.
I will sit here under the tree
and wait
until the apple falls."

The third night
a tiger came through the forest.
He saw the lion
and he saw the elephant under the tree.
He saw the golden apple shining in the moonlight.
"Am I not the strongest of all the animals?"
said the tiger.
"This apple belongs to me.
I will sit here under the tree
and wait
until the apple falls."

On the fourth night
a giraffe came through the forest.
She saw the lion,
she saw the elephant,
and she saw the tiger, all under the tree.
She saw the golden apple shining in the moonlight.
"Am I not the tallest of all the animals?"
said the giraffe.
"This apple belongs to me.
I will sit here under the tree
and wait
until the apple falls."

When the fifth night came,
a fox ran through the forest.
He saw the lion,
he saw the elephant,
he saw the tiger,
and he saw the giraffe, all under the tree.
He saw the golden apple shining in the moonlight.
"Am I not the cleverest of all the animals?"
said the fox.
"This apple belongs to me.
I will sit here under the tree
and wait
until the apple falls."

But the apple
did not fall,
and the animals under the tree
got very hungry.
Still none of them dared to leave
for fear
the apple might fall.

On the sixth night
a squirrel came through the forest.
The hungry animals
jumped at the squirrel,
and some of them would have eaten him.
But the squirrel
ran up the tree
and sat
right beside the golden apple.

The squirrel laughed and said,
"I am not a king,
I am not the largest,
I am not the strongest,
I am not the tallest,
I am not the cleverest,
yet the golden apple is mine."

But when he had nibbled through its stem,
the golden apple
was too big and too heavy
for him to hold.
It slipped through his paws
and fell to the ground.

The lion, the elephant,
the tiger, the giraffe,
and, of course, the fox, all
fell upon the apple.
And then began
a terrible fight.
There was roaring and shouting
and biting and slapping,
until the five big animals forgot
all about the golden apple.
They ran off howling.

The lion was bleeding.
The elephant had lost a tooth.
The tiger saw with only one eye.
The giraffe could hear with only one ear.
The fox was limping.

And the squirrel ran away, too.
He had decided he did not need the golden apple.
He was happy enough without it.

On the seventh night,
lost in the forest,
came a child like you.
The child walked through the forest
and found by the tree
the golden apple.

ISBN 0 370 01536 3
Copyright © 1970 by Artemis Verlag, Zurich
English text copyright © 1970 by Atheneum Publishers, Inc. New York
Printed in Switzerland by Lichtdruck AG, Dielsdorf ·
for The Bodley Head Ltd
9 Bow Street, London WC2
First published in Great Britain 1970